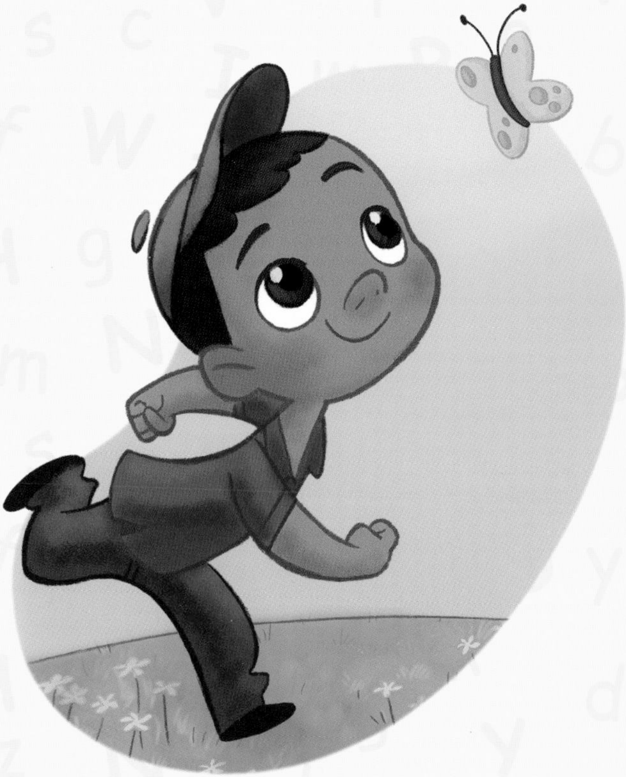

Published by Age of Learning, Inc., P.O. Box 10458, Glendale, California 91209.
No part of this work may be reproduced in whole or in part, or stored in a retrieval system,
or transmitted in any form or by any means, electronic, mechanical, photocopying,
recording, or otherwise, without written permission of the publisher.
ABCmouse.com and associated logos are trademarks and/or
registered trademarks of Age of Learning, Inc.

Library of Congress Cataloging-in-Publication Data
To Run Is Fun/Age of Learning, Inc.
Summary: In this Word Family Beginning Reader, a little boy likes to run,
but on a rainy day he has to wait.

ISBN: 978-1-62116-010-6
Library of Congress Control Number: 2012912285

21 20 19 18 17 16 15 14 13 12   1 2 3 4 5
Printed in the U.S.A., on 10% recycled paper. ♻
First printing, December 2012

To Run is Fun

Age of Learning, Inc., Glendale, California
This book is also available at **ABCmouse.com**, the award-winning early learning online curriculum.
Find free apps at **ABCmouse.com/apps**.

I like to run.
To run is fun!
All day long.
I run, run, run!

I like to run
out in the sun.
When there is sun,
it's fun, fun, fun!

I eat a hot dog in a bun. Then I go out and run, run, run!

If it rains,
I do not run.
I do not run
without the sun!

One day, I saw there was no sun. That day, I did not run, run, run!

I sat all day.
It was not fun.
It is more fun
to run, run, run!

I ate a hot dog in a bun. I waited for the sun, sun, sun!

The sun came out.
Now I can run.
I run so fast!
To run is fun!